Blazing Balloon

The marvelous Montgolfier brothers built the first hot-air balloon over 200 years ago. Rising hot air filled the balloon, lifting its passengers up, up, and away!

Complete the other half of the balloon, then color it in.

Now color these famous flying machines!

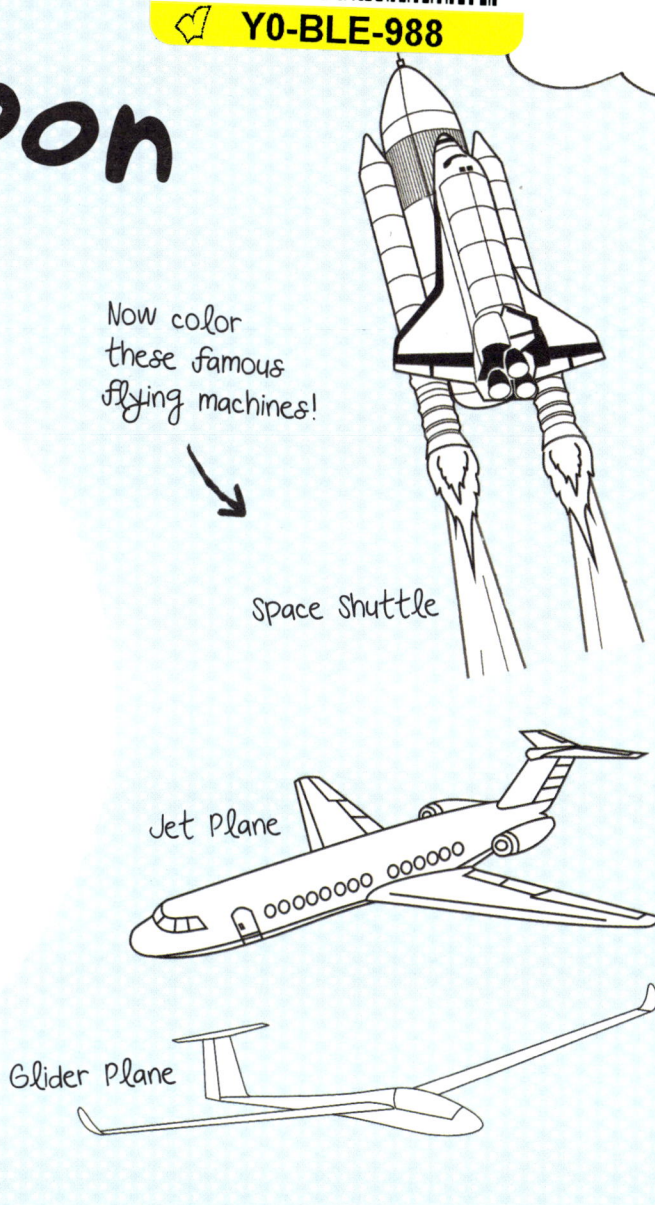

Space Shuttle

Jet Plane

Glider Plane

Helicopter

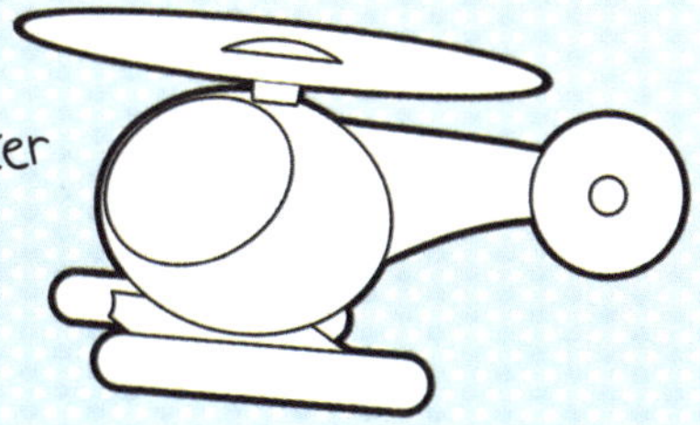

DID YOU KNOW?
The Montgolfier Brothers' balloon was painted sky blue and gold, and included animals and zodiac signs in its design.

The Perfect Picnic

These picnickers are having a whale of a time! Complete the scene and plan your perfect picnic sandwich below.

Is it a sunny or rainy day?

Add a balloon to the string.

Plant a tall tree here.

Draw some delicious veggies growing here.

Who is this robin talking to?

What snacks are in the picnic basket?

Check the ingredients for your ultimate sandwich. Add your own if they are not on the list!

- cheese ☐
- ham ☐
- lettuce ☐
- tomato ☐
- onion ☐
- olives ☐
- pickles ☐
- pepperoni ☐
- hummus ☐
- chicken ☐
- peppers ☐
- cucumber ☐
- tuna ☐
- egg ☐

....
....

Monkey Business

Color the shapes with an "x" BROWN to show an animal having a swinging good time!

Color all the other shapes in different shades of GREEN.

Now color in the rest of these rain-forest creatures!

TABLE TICKLER

How do monkeys get down the stairs?

They slide down the banana-ster!

Cool Pool

Doodle some designs on these lounge chairs.

These friends are staying cool in the pool. Draw more summery stuff to make a real splash!

Add some ice cream cones and popsicles to the tray.

Why not draw yourself here?

Who's coming down the slide?

Give this girl something cool to drink!

Add a beach ball here.

Copy this sandcastle into the grid next to it. Try drawing one square at a time, then give your picture some color!

DID YOU KNOW?

The largest sandcastle ever built was almost 38 feet (11 meters) tall! Around 1,500 volunteers helped build it in over 2,500 work hours. That's quite an effort!

The Big Bang

The Big Bang is what happened when our universe began—more than 13 billion years ago! Color in the almighty explosion using the colored dots as a guide.

The astronaut and the alien are partying—outer space style! What do you think they are saying? What language can the alien speak? Fill in the speech balloons.

Meet Mona Lisa

Legendary artist Leonardo da Vinci painted the Mona Lisa with a mysterious smile on her face.

Try giving the painting a twist by changing Mona Lisa's expression!

What has amused my muse?

- tickled
- angry
- frightened
- embarrassed

Who are all these people staring at me?

DID YOU KNOW?
The Mona Lisa, the world's most famous portrait can be found in the Louvre art gallery in Paris, France.

Which other one of these famous sights is also located in Paris? Circle the correct picture!

Now color in the stunning sight you would most like to visit.

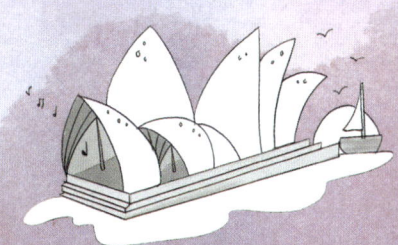

- Opera House
- Big Ben
- Eiffel Tower
- Statue of Liberty

Answer: the Eiffel Tower is in Paris.

Space Race

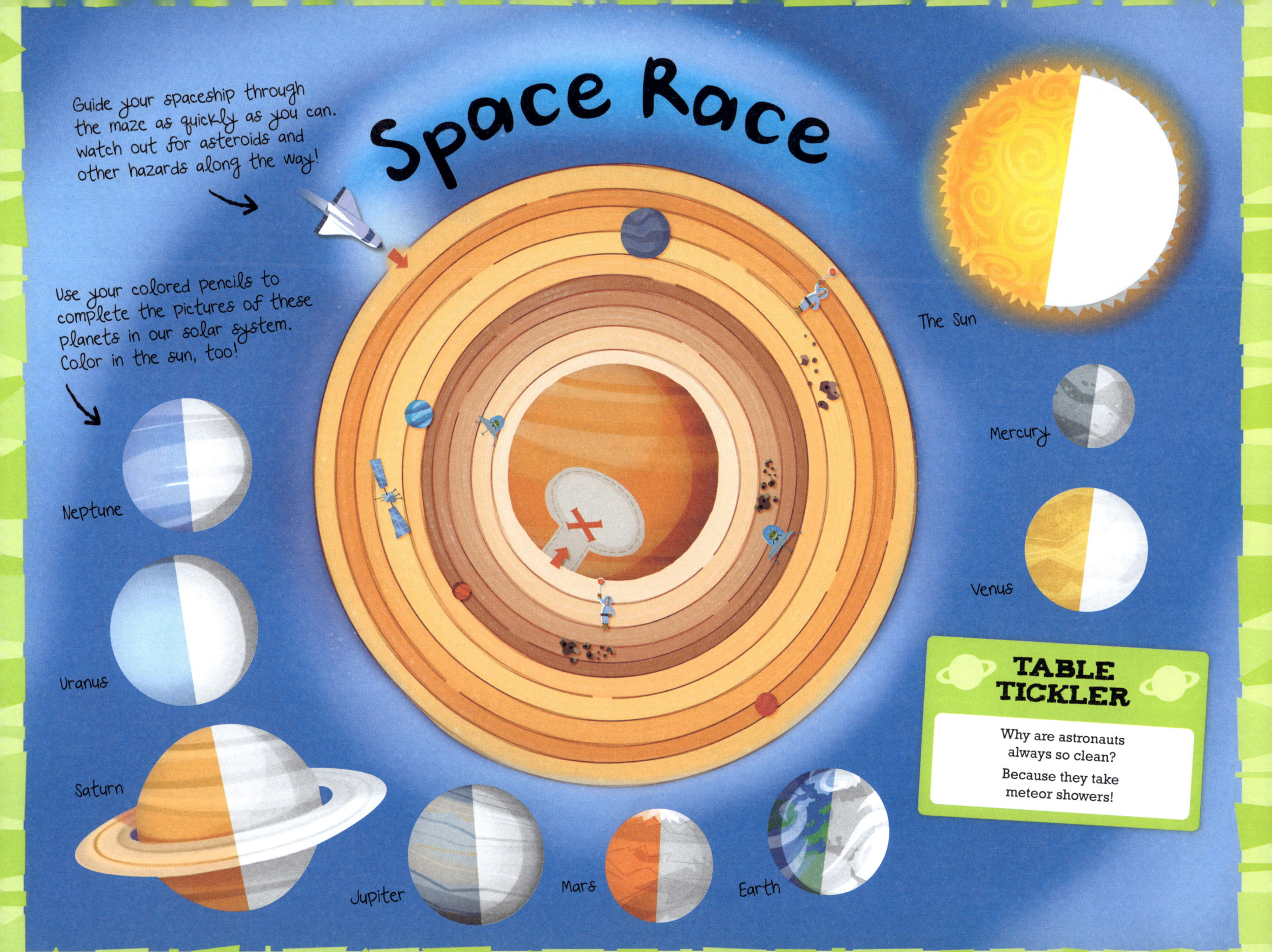

Guide your spaceship through the maze as quickly as you can. Watch out for asteroids and other hazards along the way!

Use your colored pencils to complete the pictures of these planets in our solar system. Color in the sun, too!

Neptune

Uranus

Saturn

Jupiter

Mars

Earth

The Sun

Mercury

Venus

TABLE TICKLER

Why are astronauts always so clean?

Because they take meteor showers!

Favorite Foods

Draw in all your favorite meals.

Yummy breakfast

Favorite lunch

Best dessert

DID YOU KNOW?
Pizza has been eaten for thousands of years! Even the ancient Greeks liked to eat flatbread topped with herbs, onion, and garlic.

Add some delicious toppings to this pizza. Can you draw the ingredients in a pattern that makes you smile?

MY FAVORITE PIZZA FLAVOR IS
....

Hatching Dragons

This special dragon egg is due to hatch any day! But how many baby dragons are sharing a shell?

These dragons have all lost something shiny. Follow the lines to see which dragon owns which fine treasure.

1. Nice-but-dim Dragon
2. Lesser-spotted Lizardface
3. Winged wormtail

Golden Chalice

Diamond Ring

Rare Ruby

Write the number in the box, then color each dragon a different color.

Answers: There are 5 dragons in the egg. 1. Nice-but-dim Dragon: Golden Chalice, 2. Lesser-spotted Lizardface: Rare Ruby, 3. Winged wormtail: Diamond Ring.

TV Dinner

Until the 1960s, television programs were all black and white. Today's TVs are super slim and show pictures in color, High Definition, and even 3D!

What is this family watching?
Choose a TV show, then draw a scene on the screen.

1 SPORT
2 PETS
3 NATURE
4 COOKING
5 CARTOONS
6 NEWS

Funny Phones

The very first person to make a phone call was its inventor, Alexander Graham Bell, in 1876! The telephone has changed a lot since then.

Think of something funny for these four people to say.

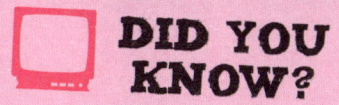

1910
1930
1980
2014

DID YOU KNOW?

In Japan almost all cell phones are waterproof. People can take them in the shower!

A Pirate's Life

Color in these pictures and mark your favorite pirate job with a star. Which pirate would you not want to be? Make a cross next to the picture.

CAPTAIN
(gets the most treasure!)

FIRST MATE
(boss of the ship when the captain is on land!)

GUNNER
(in charge of the cannon)

SURGEON
(fixes up pirates after sword fights)

STOWAWAY
(not an official crew member!)

CABIN BOY
(generally handy)

Do you have what it takes to join this terrifying pirate crew? Draw yourself in pirate dress here. You could wear an eye patch, bandana, and even have a parrot on your shoulder.

DID YOU KNOW?

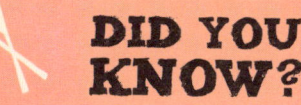

Pirates often carried parrots because they were worth a whole lot of gold! These exotic birds were also used to bribe officials, but mainly they were good company.

Vantastic

Draw a child riding a bicycle here.

DID YOU KNOW?
The VW camper van celebrated its 60th birthday in 2010. That's probably quite a bit older than your parents!

Add some trees for scenery... or even a beach!

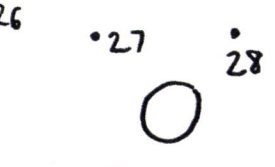

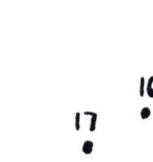

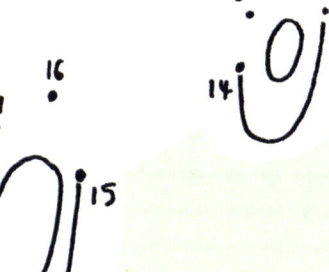

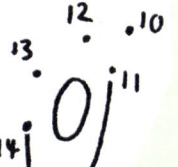

Join the dots to reveal a cool camper van rolling down the road. Then color it in!

Where is the van heading? Draw a road sign!

Draw a delicious dessert in this sundae glass. Add scoops of ice cream, your favorite sauce, fruit, sprinkles, and wafers!

Create a Cyborg

This cyborg is feeling incomplete! Using your best robotic skills, copy the cyborg parts to where you think they belong on his body. Then color in your creation.

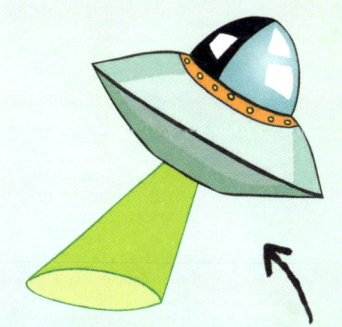

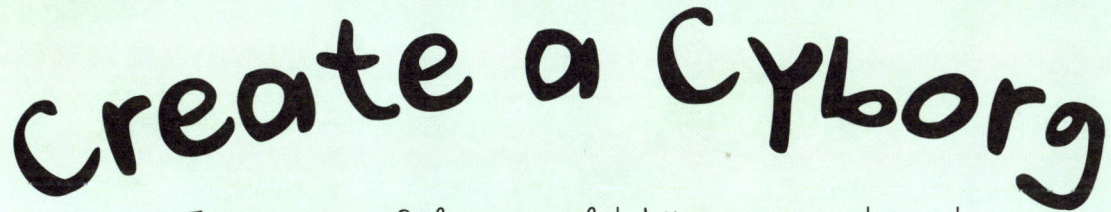

There is only one other spaceship on this page that exactly matches this one. Draw a circle around it when you find it.

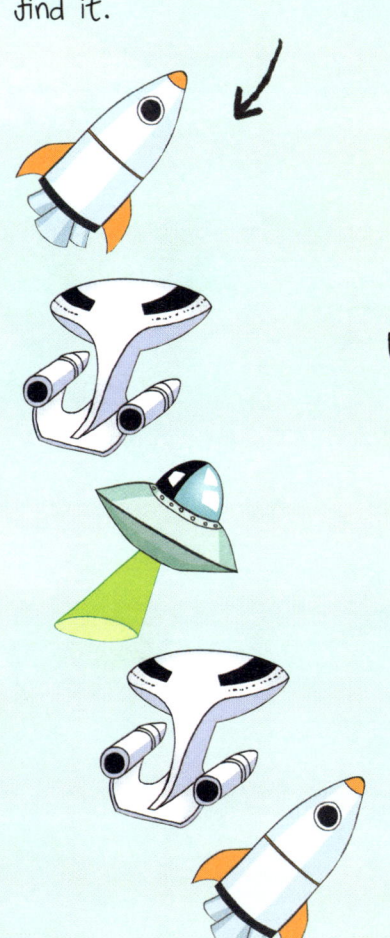

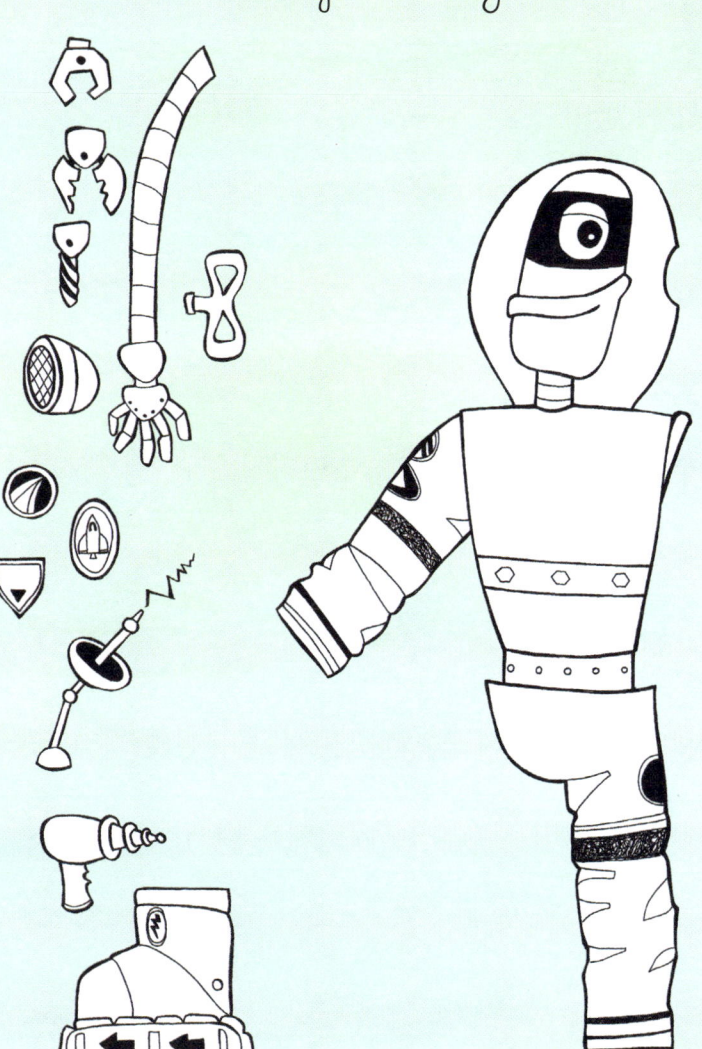

What's a robot's favorite type of music?

Heavy metal!

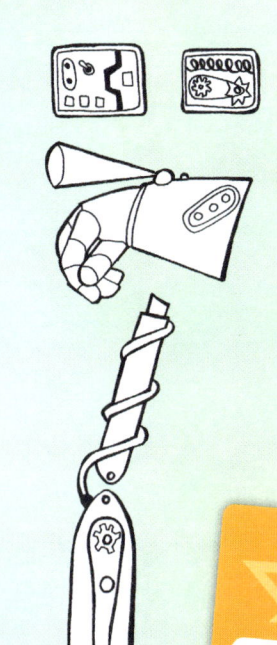

DID YOU KNOW?

A cyborg is a human being who has had some of his or her body parts replaced with robotic ones! That's out of this world!

Sunny Shores

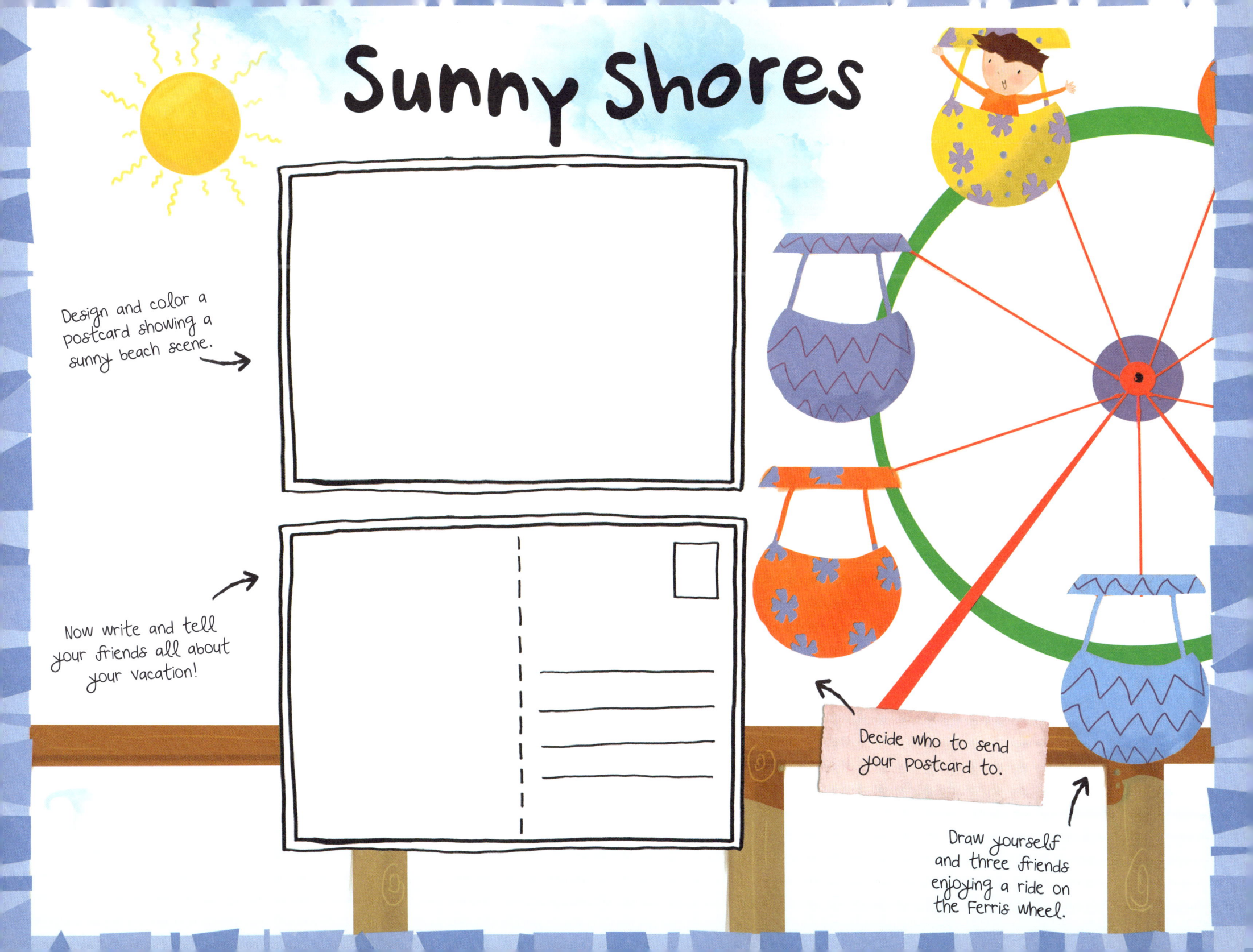

Design and color a postcard showing a sunny beach scene.

Now write and tell your friends all about your vacation!

Decide who to send your postcard to.

Draw yourself and three friends enjoying a ride on the Ferris wheel.

Amazing Artist

Amaze your friends and family with your artistic flair. Finish the pictures in this gallery.

Italian artist Giuseppe Arcimboldo painted this frame of fruit. Now turn the page upside down to see a new picture magically appear!

FRUIT BASKET...

...OR FUNNY FACE?

Add a bouquet of flowers to this ancient vase.

A beautiful landscape.

Me by me!

Draw your self-portrait. (Try using a mirror or a photo of yourself.)

Give these lines and shapes some color.

Draw a proud prince or princess in the frame.

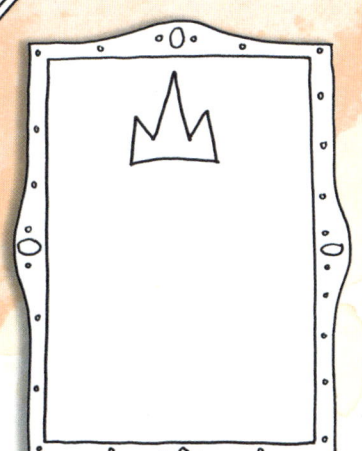

Draw your most monstrous creation here.

Star Gazing

Take a closer look through the telescope. Can you spot five differences between the pictures?

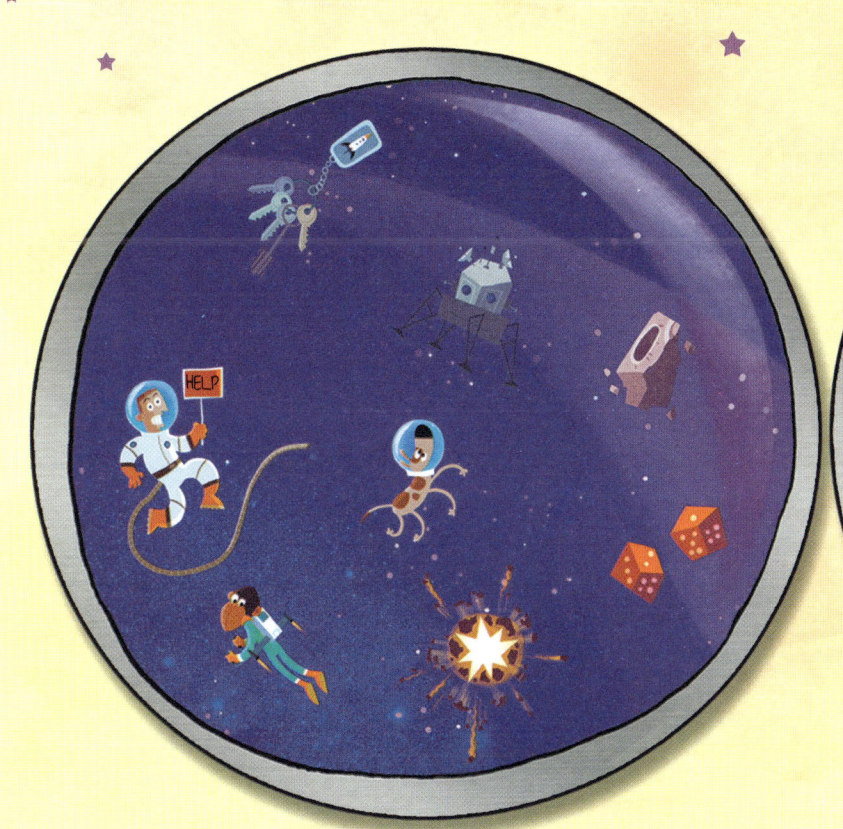

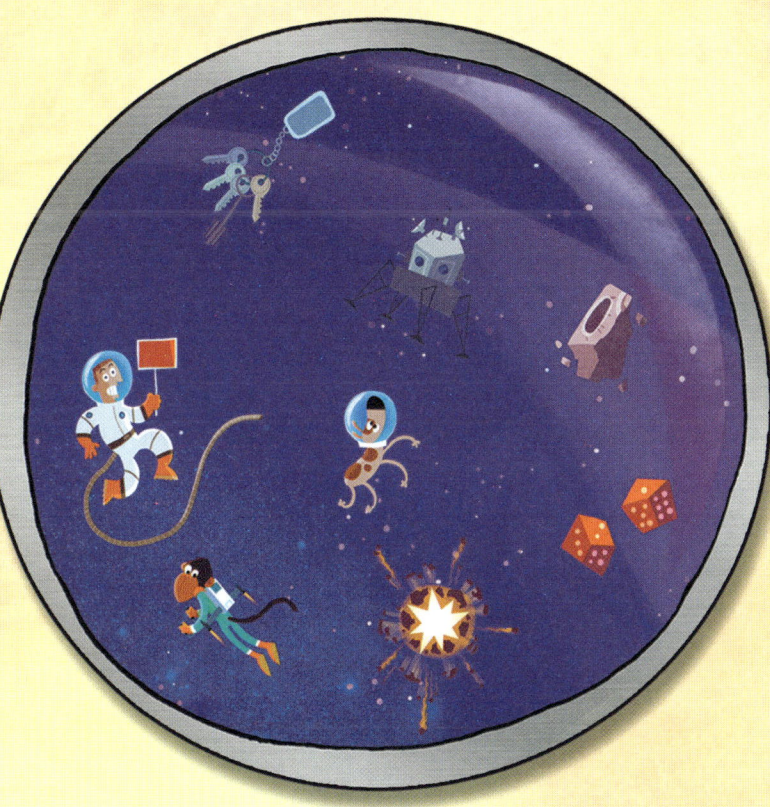

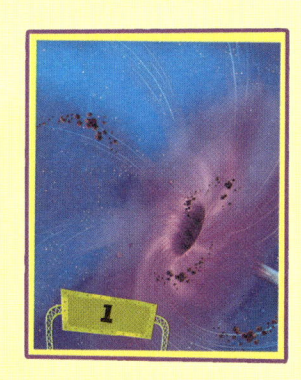

Red Alert! Which of these black holes is the odd one out?

1 2 3 4 5 6

Telescope answers: The keyring doesn't have a rocket on it, the monkey grew a tail, the astronaut's sign doesn't say HELP, the dog's tail has gone missing, the die has changed from four to six on one side.
Red Alert answer: black hole 4 is the odd one out.

Fabulous Face

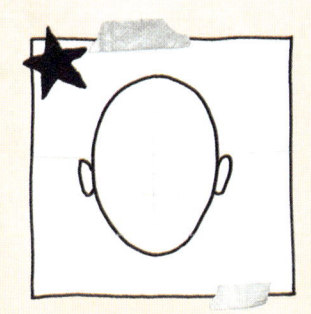

Draw an oval face shape and two ears. Add faint guidelines.

Good start!

Draw eyebrows in line with the tops of the ears, then add a pair of eyes.

Keep on going!

Add a nose – big or small. Draw it in line with the bottom of the ears.

Top drawing!

Now add a smile and design a cool hairstyle.

How handsome!

DID YOU KNOW?

Before photography was invented, drawing or painting portraits was the only way to record pictures of people. Only the rich could afford their own portraits.

Which new colors do these paints make when mixed together?

1. 🔴 + 🟡 = ☐
2. ⚪ + ⚫ = ☐
3. 🔵 + ☐ = 🟣
4. ☐ + 🔴 = 🟠
5. ☐ + 🔵 = 🟢

Answer: The missing colors are: 1. Orange, 2. Gray, 3. Red, 4. Yellow, 5. Yellow.

Ship Ahoy!

HARRRR YE BE FUNNY!
Why couldn't the pirate play cards? Because he was standing on the deck!

Make someone walk the plank!

Draw the ship's captain at the helm.

Draw a Jolly Roger here.

Doodle a pirate pair here.

Add some prisoners below deck.

BOOM! Fire a cannonball from the cannon!

Someone's gone for a swim.

Add a shark.

MOTLEY CREW
Create your own crew by giving them colorful hats, beards, and earrings. Give them names, too!

.... THE FEARSOME

GREEDY ....

CABIN GIRL ....

On A Safari

Make the sun shine.

Which predator has spotted these zebras?

Draw an animal with a long neck looking for its lunch.

Doodle the plants and animals that these adventurers can see from their tour bus.

Copy one of the trees here.

Color in this tourist!

Add a couple of baby meerkats. So cute!

Add a giant bug here.

Bring some color to the side of the tour bus.

TABLE TICKLER

What do you call an elephant that never washes?

A smellyphant!

THIS NATURE RESERVE IS CALLED
....

Sea monster makeovers

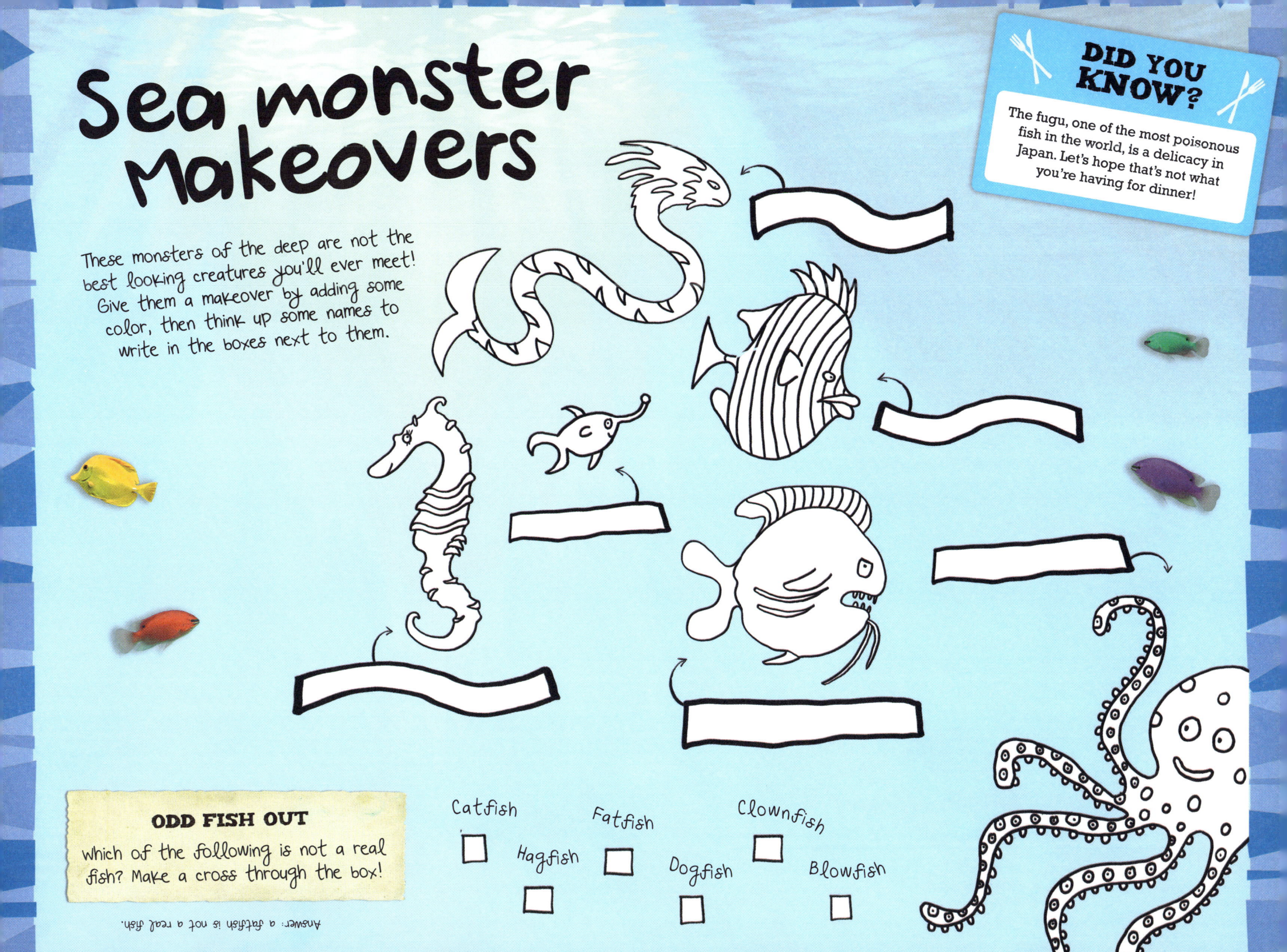

These monsters of the deep are not the best looking creatures you'll ever meet! Give them a makeover by adding some color, then think up some names to write in the boxes next to them.

DID YOU KNOW?
The fugu, one of the most poisonous fish in the world, is a delicacy in Japan. Let's hope that's not what you're having for dinner!

ODD FISH OUT
Which of the following is not a real fish? Make a cross through the box!

- Catfish ☐
- Hagfish ☐
- Fatfish ☐
- Dogfish ☐
- Clownfish ☐
- Blowfish ☐

Answer: a fatfish is not a real fish.

The Inventions Lab

Here's your chance to create some incredible inventions! What will you dream up?

DID YOU KNOW?
The microwave was invented by accident! While developing a complicated magnet machine, a chocolate bar melted in the inventor's pocket.

Create some more cogs and whirring wheels.

This invention could change the world!

What is your latest invention? Draw it here.

Draw yourself wearing an inventor's lab coat.

Draw some test tubes and beakers on the shelves.

What is this inventor's idea?

Guide the pirate raft safely through the shark-infested waters to reach dry land.

Scary Sharks

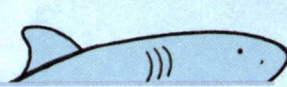

CHECK THE THINGS A PIRATE NEEDS TO SAIL THE SEVEN SEAS.

Which thing does a pirate not *usually* need to cross the seven seas? Put a check in the box next to it.

DID YOU KNOW?

As you read this, around 20 volcanoes are erupting all over the world! You can find volcanoes on land, on the ocean floor, and even under icebergs.

Imagine that you owned a wildlife park where people could marvel at the animals and plants. Write here what it would be like!

Wildlife Park

These parrots have beautiful feathers! Color the bottom image to match the top one.

My biggest animal would be a ....

My fiercest animal would be a ....

My most poisonous animal would be a ....

My smallest animal would be a ....

My noisiest animal would be a ....

My prettiest animal would be a ....

At the Movies

When the Lumière Brothers put on their first movie show in 1895, it was only shown in black and white and had no sound!

Draw and color your favorite movie character here.

Follow the tangled headphone wires to discover when these audio devices were invented.

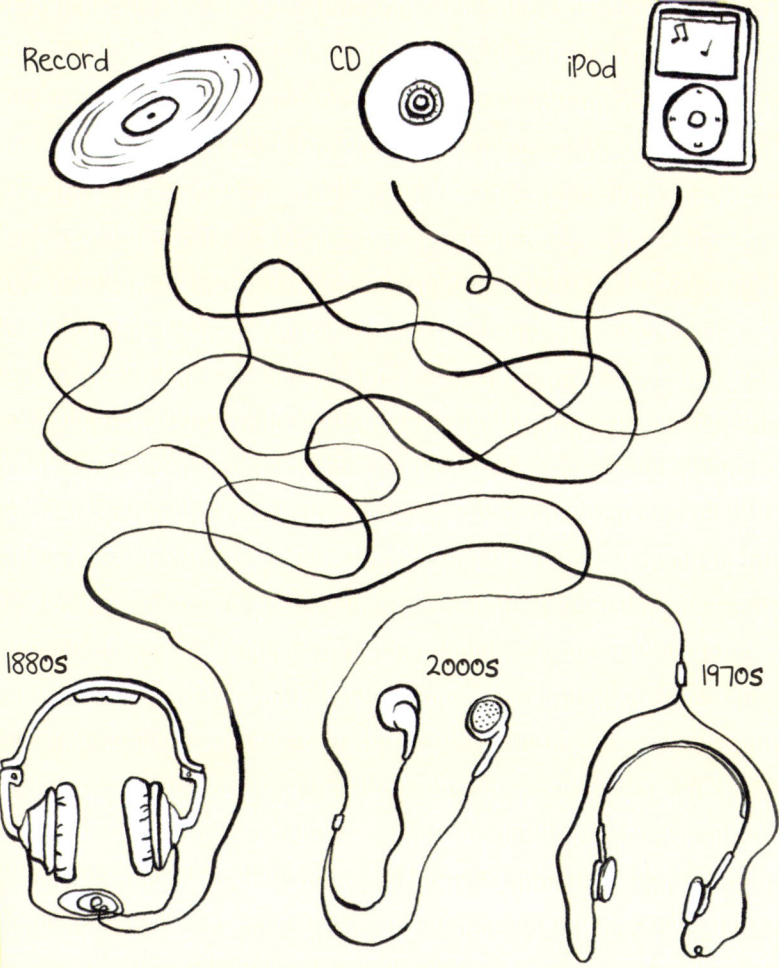

Record   CD   iPod

1880s   2000s   1970s

DID YOU KNOW?

Popcorn became the most popular movie munchie in the 1920s, as it was a cheap snack that moviegoers could afford during the Great Depression. Munch!

Answers: Record: 1880s, CD: 1970s, iPod: 2000s.

Pirate Dress-up

Draw some perfect pirate outfits on the clothes line!

TABLE TICKLER

What is a pirate's favorite subject at school?

Arrrrrrrithmetic!

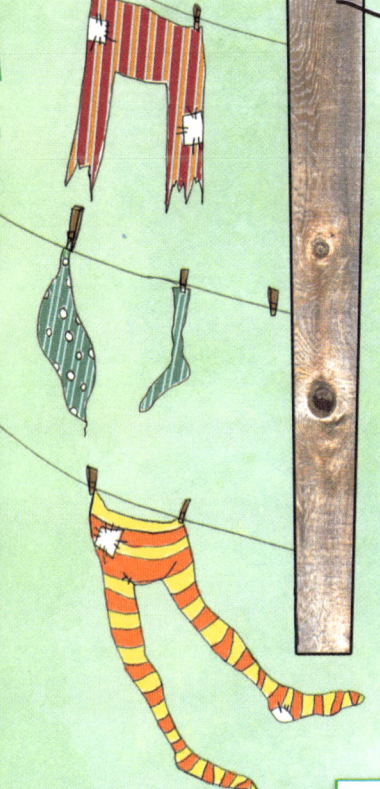

↑ T-SHIRT

↑ BANDANA

↑ SHORTS

↑ SUN HAT AND SWIM TRUNKS

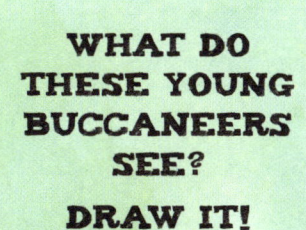

WHAT DO THESE YOUNG BUCCANEERS SEE? DRAW IT!

Beach Fun

Color in the shapes with a dot inside to uncover a secret shape in the sand.

Study these seaside scenes. Can you spot five differences between the pictures?

Answer: the blonde girl's sunglasses are missing, the shovel has changed color, the stripe on the pail has disappeared, the wave has changed shape, an extra flag has appeared on the sandcastle.

Launch Time

When does an astronaut eat?
At launch time!
Doodle a delicious dinner
for this hungry space explorer.

APPETIZER

DRINK

MAIN COURSE

DESSERT

THE ASTRO AGENCY

1. ....
2. ....
3. ....
4. ....
5. ....
6. ....

Make a list of the items you would bring into space with you. Don't forget your favorite teddy bear!

DID YOU KNOW?

Most of the food on space shuttles is dried and vacuum-packed so it doesn't go bad. Astronauts have to add water to their dinner before eating it. Delicious!

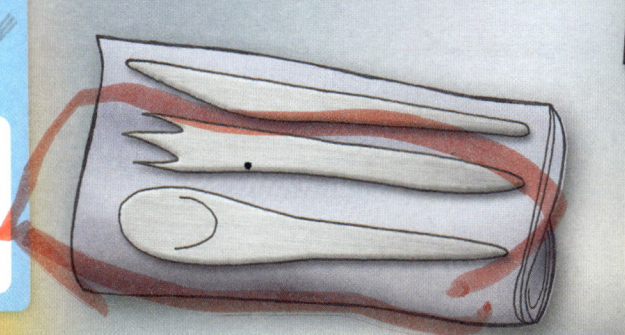

Bird Buddy

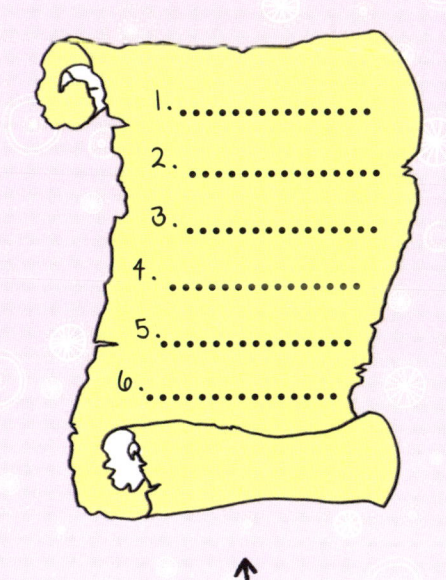

1. ....
2. ....
3. ....
4. ....
5. ....
6. ....

Copy the pirate items here in alphabetical order. Then color them in!

Color in the shapes with a dot in red to reveal a pretty Polly!

EYE PATCH

GALLEON

ISLAND

HOOK

CANNON

TREASURE CHEST

Answer: cannon, eye patch, galleon, hook, island, treasure chest.

DID YOU KNOW?

Pirates wore earrings because they believed it would make them see better.

Vacation Fun

Pack your suitcase, it's time to go on vacation!

Where is your dream destination? Write in the names of the seven continents, then draw a red circle on the map to show where you'd like to go.

AFRICA
SOUTH AMERICA
ASIA
EUROPE
AUSTRALIA
NORTH AMERICA
ANTARCTICA

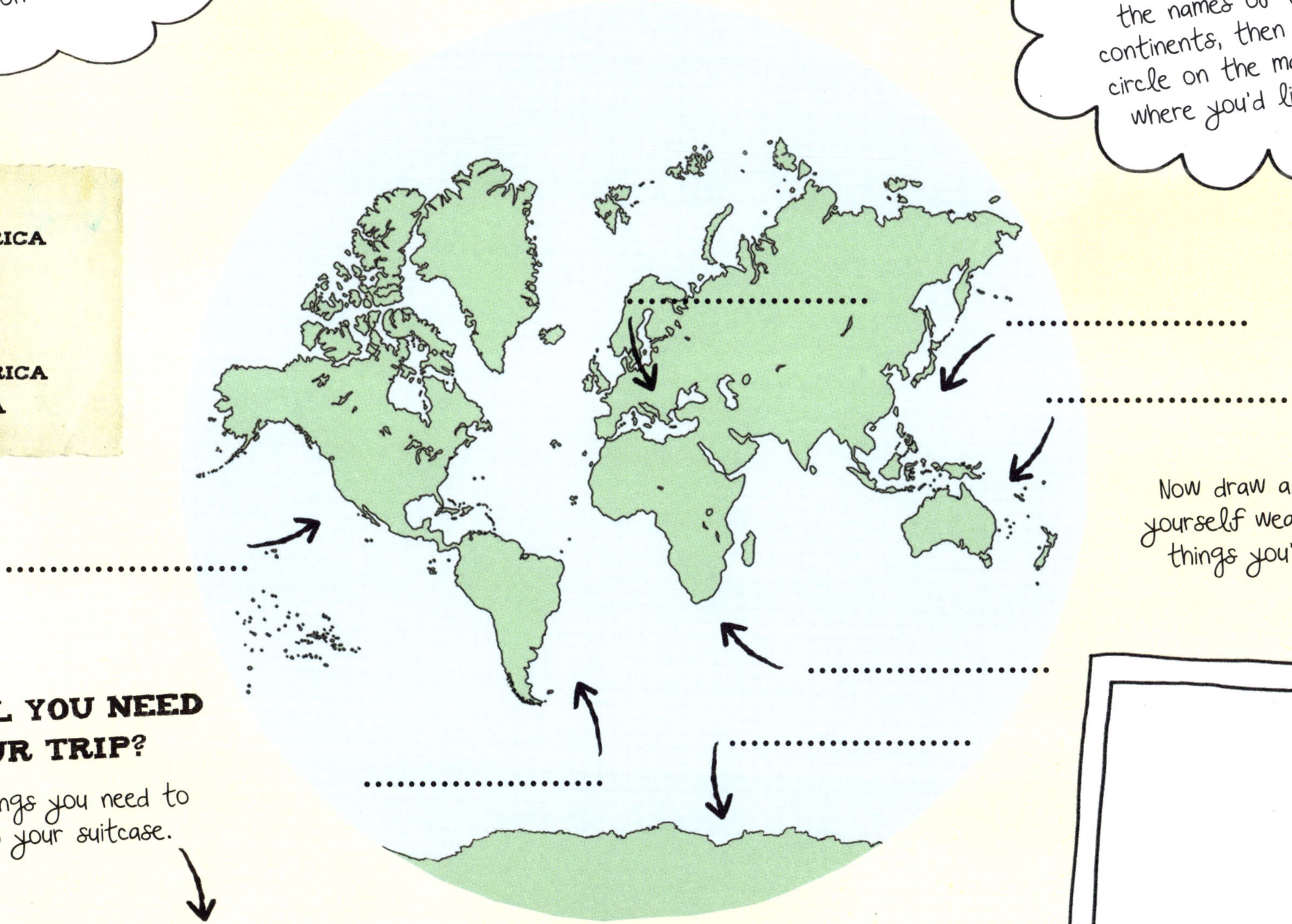

Now draw a picture of yourself wearing all the things you've packed!

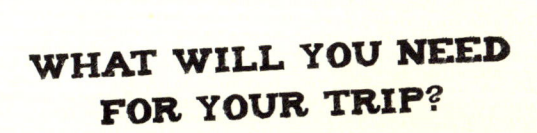

WHAT WILL YOU NEED FOR YOUR TRIP?

Check the things you need to squeeze into your suitcase.

Having a Blast

Draw a rocket on the launch pad, ready to blast into outer space!

5 4 3 2 1

BLAST OFF!

Draw in the details to complete the other half of this astronaut's outfit. Then color it in!

DID YOU KNOW?

The Soviet Union launched a rocket with the world's first man-made satellite on board almost 60 years ago. Now around 3,000 satellites orbit the Earth!

Knights and Dragons

This knight is feeling the heat! Color in the fire-breathing dragon and the daring knight using the colors in the code below.

Now color in these dragony drawings in the colors you like!

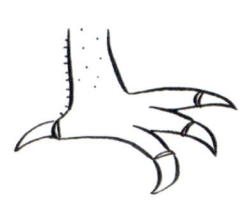

write who you think will be victorious!

....

COLOR CODE:

1 = RED   3 = PURPLE   5 = ORANGE   7 = BROWN
2 = BLUE 4 = GREEN   6 = YELLOW

Explorer Wanted

DID YOU KNOW?
A raging rhino can charge at speeds of up to 43 miles (70 km) per hour! WHOA!

What would your perfect day on a safari be like? Write it down here!

....
....
....
....
....
....
....
....

Trek through this grassland maze taking care to avoid any predators on your way.

START

FINISH

Can you fill in the missing letters to complete these animal names? Look at the maze again if you need help!

1. H Y _ _ A
2. Z E _ R _
3. _ _ R _ F F _
4. _ _ _ K _
5. A _ T _ L O P E
6. _ I O _
7. _ E E _ _ _ _

Answers: 1. HYENA, 2. ZEBRA, 3. GIRAFFE, 4. SNAKE, 5. ANTELOPE, 6. LION, 7. MEERKAT

Perfectly Pretty

DID YOU KNOW?
Orchids were once the most expensive flowers in the world. In the 1800s orchid hunters risked their lives trying to collect them. Disease, cannibals, and natural disasters were common hazards!

Color the matching pairs of bees in the same color so you have three pairs in total.

Color in this rare orchid, matching the numbers to these colors:

1 = pink
2 = yellow
3 = red
4 = light green
5 = dark green
6 = orange

Porthole Pirates

Now look through these portholes to see what the pirates are up to on their day off.

Check the pirate activities you would like to try. Draw a skull and crossbones by your favorite thing to do!

These pirates are definitely staying below deck! Join the dots to reveal what they have seen through the porthole.

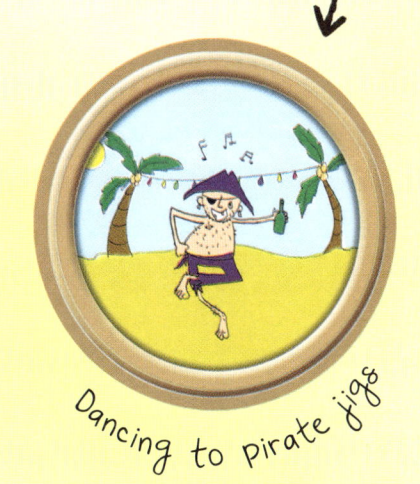

Snoozing in hammocks

Dancing to pirate jigs

Dolphin riding

Practicing sword fighting

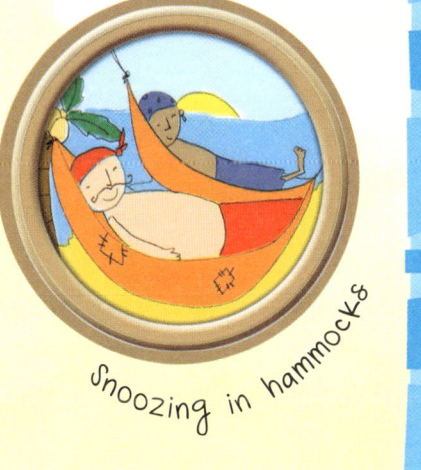

Sunny surfing

Answer: the pirates have spotted a shark.

Groovy Gadgets

Draw lines to match up the old and new inventions that do the same job!

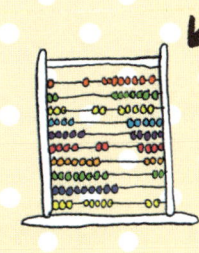

Design a fabulous new range of cell phone cases. Leave some text messages on them, too.

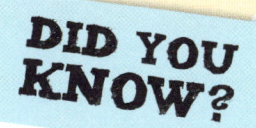

DID YOU KNOW?

The first cell phone call was made in 1973—from a phone the size of a shoe!

Unusual sights

Hang on a minute, one of these animals doesn't belong here! Do you know which one?

Draw an extinct or imaginary animal in this space.

This animal is called a ....!

Answer: The polar bear